SURF STORIES FROM THE BOARD RACK

ORDER OF CONTENTS

GH00985726

Acknowledgements

I would like to dedicate this book to my mum and her husband Rich (the legend) to my girlfriend Catherine, Tallulah, Kanace, Kacey and Riley.

And to my old surfing friends, Jools (the king of Saunton Sands) who is a true water man and Cliff Tattersall, Greg Robinson and Ashley Braunton who I have shared many waves and memories with.

Also a big thanks to the sponsor of this print edition Pete Sawyer of Kitemare Surf & Kite Shop, Westward Ho!

Trust In Magic

Tim was a happy young boy. He lived in a house with his mum and dad next to the sea. His dad was a lifeguard, and his mum ran the cafe on the beach.

What made Tim such a happy boy was the sea. Each day he would have an adventure, each day he would meet new people and make new friends.

He loved to surf. His dad would teach him the basics of surfing, and then, while his dad was keeping a close-eye on him he would paddle out into the surf and surf all day long.

Tim was only ten years old, but already he could ride waves and he loved the feeling of cruising along the wave trying to stay ahead of the breaking white water. When Tim caught a good wave all the older guys who had been on the beach since Tim could remember, would cheer and hoot. Tim liked that, but Tim's favourite part of the day was going to bed!!

"That's strange!" I hear you say, most ten-year olds hate going to bed, but not Tim!!

The reason that Tim liked going to bed so much was because of his dad's stories.

Each night Tim would choose one of the surfboards from his dad's surfboard rack, and Pete (Tim's dad) would tell him a story about it.

His dad had surfed all over the world on these boards, and Tim never heard the same story twice - except one. That was Tim's favourite story. It was a story about the board Tim's father had found the day he met his wife, Tim's mum. And it went like this.....

I was surfing in Devon (where the family now lived). The surf was big and dangerous. The waves were as big as I had ever seen. In fact, they were so big that they had woken me up in my campervan where I had been sleeping in the sand dunes. The waves were making so much noise, that when I woke up I thought there had been an explosion. The van shook each time a wave broke, and I knew it was the day that I had been training for all my life.

I looked at my watch, and saw that it was 6am. I went for a walk to the beach, and couldn't believe what I saw; waves the size of a small house coming in and breaking on the rocks. My mouth was suddenly dry and I felt nervous.

Back at the campervan I made breakfast. Sandy, (my dog) sensed that something big was going to happen, and as soon as we had eaten breakfast he ran off.

I hunted for Sandy for a while and then gave up, when a dog doesn't want to be found you won't find it.

Back at the van I got my surfboard ready. I took my time checking the leash (which attaches the board to your leg), and waxing down the deck of the board so I would get good grip when I stood up.

I put my wetsuit on, and did a nice long warm up, stretching my arms and legs. I was ready at last. I put a bowl of water down for Sandy, and walked to the beach with the ground shaking under my feet. I wondered if I would ever see my trusty dog again.

I had two choices. Paddle out through the white water, or walk along the cliff and jump off the end. I watched the sea moving for ages, and finally decided to do the cliff jump.

I fastened the leash to my ankle, prayed that I would live to tell the tale, and peered over the edge of the cliff.

The sea was angry and restless. Huge chunks of white water were popping up and forming into monster waves all over the place, and the sea seemed so far below me!!

Here goes, and with that I jumped holding my board next to me. As I landed I threw the board away from me, and that was the last I ever saw of it - the leash had snapped!

So there I was, twelve to fifteen foot waves between me and the beach, and no board to keep me afloat. The first rule of surfing, never surf alone. Now I knew why!!

I tried to swim in with the monster waves, but each time I got close to the beach the waves that had pushed me in sucked me back out to sea.

Well Tim, I have to say that I thought that was it! I was running out of energy, and getting no nearer to the beach.

I decided to swim back out to sea past all the waves where I hopefully could float around a bit and get some energy back.

I made it out through the waves with the last of my strength. I lay there floating on my back, scared, tired, frightened and all on my own.

I thought things couldn't get any worse, when to my horror I saw a shape swimming through the water. I thought it looked like a big shark or a dolphin, but then I realised that it wasn't a shark or a dolphin.

Do you know what it was?

It was a bright red gun (which is a special type of surfboard designed for surfing really big waves) I swam over to it and climbed on.

Two things crossed my mind, firstly, where was the board's owner, and secondly how lucky I was.

I looked at the board more closely, and saw the picture on the deck - A VW camper van inside a big hollow wave. The van was the same colour as my VW camper van, and under the van were the words, "TRUST IN MAGIC" and after in smaller words "You get what you give, give what you get"
Cool, I thought, hope the owner of this board is ok. I better paddle back to the beach now and tell the coastguard about the missing person.

I started paddling the new board back towards the beach, and I noticed that it felt strange. Not because it was the first time I had paddled it, but because I felt at home and at ease on it. Normally a board takes some getting used to, but this one felt like I had owned it forever!

I stroked for the biggest wave of my life, and felt the wave catch me. Up I jumped to my feet, and the drop down the wave seemed to last forever. I screamed along the wave, sure that the fins must surely slip out of the face and send me spinning off the board, but luckily they held in, and before I knew it I had ridden the biggest wave of my life all the way to the beach!!

As I scrambled my way out of the sea Sandy came running over to me and started barking. Then he shook off his wet fur right next to me, and stood looking at me with his head cocked at an angle.

I shouted at Sandy, and then made a run for the van to get changed and call the coastguard about the poor person who had lost their surfboard.

As I was peeling my wetsuit off I saw movement out of the corner of my eye. I looked up into the most beautiful eyes I had ever seen. They were the colour of water in Cornwall in the summer, clear and blue and pure. We looked at each other for a few seconds, and then the lady said,
"You've got my surfboard there, I think you should keep it, you did very well on it"

I found out that she had lost it a week before trying to learn to surf, and hadn't tried since.

In the end, Tim, I told her that I would teach her to surf, and one thing led to another, and to cut a long story short, we got married and had you, and the rest is history:- Oh, and we called you Tim because of what it said on the surf board that saved my life and started yours: Trust In Magic - TIM.

'You like that story, don't you Tim?' 'Tim?' 'Tim?'

But Tim didn't reply; he was already asleep, dreaming of surfing big waves.

Trust In Magic

The Rescue Board

Tim and Pete had been swimming in the sea, doing some lifeguard training. When they got out of the water Tim noticed a large white scar that ran from Pete's elbow all the way up to his shoulder.

"Dad, how did you get that massive scar all the way down your arm?" asked Tim.

"From my rescue board Tim, the first time I ever rescued anyone using it."

"Tell me what happened, Dad" pleaded Tim jumping up and down thinking he was going to get to hear one of his Dad's stories.

"Ok son, but not til bedtime. Now go and play while I set up the lifeguard station for the day."

All morning Tim kept getting under his Dad's feet, knocking things over, and generally being a nuisance.

"Tim! Why don't you just go for a nice long surf?" suggested Pete.

Tim went off and had a surf. The waves were super small and Tim soon got bored. He sat on his surfboard bobbing up and down on the ocean wondering how his dad got such a big scar.

I bet it was a shark bite, or a sea monster thought Tim, or no, perhaps he had to rescue people from a ship, and he used his arm to plug a hole in the side of the ship to stop them from sinking. Tim's imagination knew no limits, and time quickly passed by.

Soon enough Tim's mum was waving her towel from the top of the beach. Time to go home for supper, and then bed, thought Tim. GREAT!!

Tim's mum had made Tim's favourite for supper, bangers and mash, but Tim wolfed it down in seconds.

"I'm tired mum," said Tim rubbing his little eyes. "I'm going to bed now, goodnight."

"Goodnight sweetheart," smiled Mary, looking at her watch, "You must be tired, it's only 6.45!!"

"Yes, Oh mum," paused Tim "can you send Dad up for my story?"

"Ha! Ha!" laughed Mary, "I will see what I can do."

And with that Tim leapt up the stairs.

Pete opened Tim's bedroom door.

"Your mother says you are too tired for a bedtime story tonight."

Tim was just about to protest, when he saw the twinkle in his father's eye.

"Dad, can you tell me about the rescue board, and how you got that massive scar please?"

"Ok, you get comfy then little man, and I will tell you all about it".

"Well Tim, it all happened two weeks after I had qualified as a beach lifeguard. The weather had been getting worse all week, much to the disappointment of all the holiday makers.

It was a Thursday, and most of the holidaymakers had been visiting for nearly a week. One group of young lads had been surfing on our beach every day. They had improved quite a lot and were feeling pretty confident.

Anyway, this Thursday the head lifeguard had decided to red flag the beach, which meant in his opinion the sea was too dangerous, and you were not allowed into the water.

We put the red flags up, and put a notice by the car park saying the beach was shut.

The wind was blowing from the north, and was very cold. The sea was awash with white horses and nasty dumping waves.

Jon and I sat in the lifeguard hut drinking tea and watching the beach. I noticed the group of lads walking down from the car park with their surfboards, so we went up to them and explained what the flags meant, and told the boys to try another beach.

They argued with us for ages, trying to tell us that they would be fine, and that you could surf it easily. In the end though they agreed with us and decided to go and surf somewhere else. Jon and I went back to the hut glad to be out of the wind, and started watching the beach again.

Well those silly boys didn't go back to the car-park, they crept through the fence, walked all the way along the sand dunes down to the other end of the beach, and started surfing down there.

The sea was very restless and strong, and soon the boys were tired, but try as hard as they could they couldn't paddle back to the beach. They were caught in a rip current.

Now, all they needed to do was paddle up or down the beach for a bit, and then paddle towards the beach again and they would have got back to safety easily, but these boys weren't wise in the ways of the sea, and soon they ran out of energy.

The first Jon or I knew about it was when we saw them drifting out to sea waving for help.

Well, there were three of them and only two of us, but Jon said if we could use the rescue boards to paddle out to them we would be able to bring them back in no problem.

Now rescue boards are long and very thick surfboards, and down each of the sides (next to the rails) there are straps. People can hold on to the straps, and because the boards are so thick and floaty it is possible to rescue more than one person per board.

Jon and I paddled really hard and eventually after what seemed like hours we were with the boys.

They were very scared and cold, but before we could bring them back to the beach we had to be sure that there were only the three of them in the sea.

When we were sure I put two of them on my board, and Jon took the biggest boy, and we paddled back towards the beach.

I was very fit, and so was Jon, but even so we were both running out of energy by the time we got them to the safety of the beach.

Back at the lifeguard hut we gave them blankets and a hot drink, and slowly they warmed up and calmed down.

They said they were sorry for being so stupid, and for making us risk our lives rescuing them, and then their parents came to collect them.

At the end of the day Jon and I left work with a warm feeling inside us knowing that we had saved the lives of three boys."

"I'm going to be a lifeguard when I'm older dad," said Tim in a sleepy voice. "But what about the scar on your arm?"
Pete smiled slyly, "Tim I dropped the rescue board off the roof of the car as I was strapping it down. The wind got under it, and the fin gashed my arm as I tried to catch it. Please don't mention exactly how I got the scar. Some people have heard a different story, something about fighting a shark. Now I don't know how these rumours started, (Tim had a fair idea!) but it would be a shame to disappoint your mother and everyone else, so let's not spoil it for them, ok partner?"

"Ok Dad," grinned Tim, and Pete and Tim shook hands in the surfers hand shake and winked at each other.

As Pete stood up and walked towards the door he looked back, but his son was already fast asleep, no doubt dreaming of the people he would rescue when he became a beach lifeguard too.

The Paddleboard Race

"Time for bed!" called Tim's mum.
"I will send dad up for a quick story, you go ahead and brush your teeth."

"OK" said Tim, and rushed upstairs.

Tim had been waiting for half an hour for bed time. He already knew what surfboard he was going to ask his dad about tonight.

Tim's dad, Pete, crept upstairs and peeked around the bedroom door.
"Hello son, are you asleep?"
"No dad, is it story time?"
"Yes, ok, which board do you want a story about tonight?"
"Can you tell me about the one with the really big clock in the nose?"

Pete laughed and sat down on the edge of the bed.

"Ok you get comfy then little man, and I will tell you all about it.

That board is very famous, in fact that board has saved lots of people from getting hurt.

When I was twenty-four and living in my campervan I had lots of friends who lived in their vans as well. We all used to park wherever we liked and no-one gave us any trouble. We never left a mess, and if we had a fire we would always put it out, and clean it up.

The local people liked us, and we would always help all the people who lived on the boats at Velator Quay which was near where we often parked.

We made an effort to get along with all the local home owners and everything was fine.

In the summer people would come to Devon on holiday, and some would camp in their vans. We all used to get along well with no problems.

Then one summer a group of people came to surf and stayed in their vans, but they weren't so friendly.

At first things were ok, but they stayed longer than the other holiday-makers, and then things started to go wrong.

They left litter everywhere, made noise late at night, and showed no respect for the local people.

One night after a big day of surfing things got out of hand. All the people had been drinking, and when they got back to their vans someone decided to make a fire. One thing led to another and a van caught fire. The fire brigade had to come and put the fire out.

After that no-one was allowed to park their vans at Crow Point overnight.

It was a bit unfair, because all the local surfers had been careful and respectful, but we had all been tarnished with the same brush.

Some of my friends wanted to fight the Crow Pointers (as we called them), but I knew that would only make things worse.

In the end I made a deal with their leader. We would have a paddle-board race from Westward Ho! to Croyde Bay. They could choose one person, and we would choose one person, and whichever side lost would have to leave Devon!!

My friends all chose me to represent them, and a man called Rob was chosen to paddle for the Crow Pointers. We had two weeks to get ready, I had a very serious training programme to follow, and I asked my surfboard shaper to prepare a board for me designed especially for paddling.

As I chose where the race would be between, Rob decided that he should choose what time the race was to be held. Now I think that Rob knew that I was a better paddler than him, so the Crow Pointers hatched a cunning plan...they chose to run the race at night!!

They told us twenty-four hours before the race was due to start, hoping to confuse us.

I told Little Al who was making my paddleboard, and he sat for a few minutes, and then a smile slowly spread across his face. Later he gave me the board I was going to use, and on the board he had built in a compass!!

"If you get lost just paddle north, and you will end up on Croyde Beach!" smiled Little Al triumphantly.
"COOL!!" I grinned thanking Little Al for his brilliant idea.

We all drove down to the beach at 10pm for the start of the race. Rob had lights on the front of his surfboard; he even had lights on a headband so he could see where he was paddling.

The two groups of surfers stood on either side of the car park looking menacing. As the village clock struck 11pm Rob and I ran to the water's edge and began paddling.

The two groups of surfers drove round to Croyde Bay to wait and see who would arrive first, and see which group of surfers would have to move on.

After forty minutes of paddling I was about half-way, and a long way in front of the bobbing lights of Rob. I noticed a sea mist blowing in, so I speeded up, and 35 minutes later I was the winner much to the disappointment of the Crow Pointers.

We all waited on the beach for Rob, but after another hour passed he still hadn't arrived. After another half an hour I decided to paddle back and look for him.

I had been paddling for twenty minutes when I heard Rob calling out for help.

His lights had stopped working, and he had been paddling round in circles for ages!!

I paddled over to him, and told him to follow behind me holding onto my leash. I started paddling north again, and after what seemed like hours I thought I saw the glow of a fire dead ahead. Ten minutes later Rob and I were very glad to feel the sand beneath our feet, and the warm glow of a beach fire warming us up.

"How did you know where the beach was?" questioned Rob when we had warmed up a bit. "I couldn't see anything because of the fog," he added.

"That wasn't fog, it was sea mist, and when you have surfed around here for as long as I have you get to know the currents, tides and rips like the palm of your hand. I could paddle back to Croyde Bay from anywhere round here, just by feeling what the sea is doing," I lied.

"Wow!" said Rob, "you really are a proper surfer. Thanks for rescuing me; I owe you one."
After that we put more driftwood on the fire and had a party to celebrate. In the morning the Crow Pointers loaded up their vans and got ready to drive away. Before they left we told them that they could come back every year for two weeks, and then they drove off.

Now every year they come and visit, and we always have a big party on Croyde Beach. Little Al and all my friends think it's so funny that no-one has ever told Rob or the Crow Pointers about the compass, and every year Rob asks to see the board I used in the race, but I keep making up excuses, and my friends keep on laughing as Rob tells anyone who will listen how I saved his life on a dark, misty night with nothing but my paddle board and 10 years of surfing experience!!

"So Tim, if I take you to the beach party this year you won't tell will you?...Tim...Tim", but Pete didn't need to worry because Tim was sound asleep dreaming of being a hero and saving lost surfers.

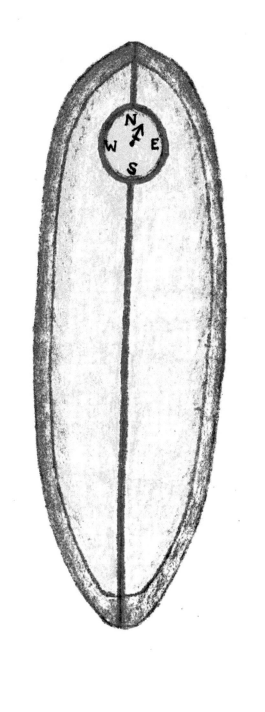

The World's First Short Board

Tim was eating his supper when his dad came back from the beach.
"Honey, why are you throwing this out?"
Pete was holding up what looked like a boogie board.

"The garage is full of junk. This is always lying on your board rack.
We need more room. What is this rubbish anyway?"

"That, babe, is not rubbish it's a piece of surfing history. If it wasn't
for that, surfing may never have progressed to where it is today"

Tim was listening, but couldn't contain his excitement anymore.

"Dad, why is it so special? Will you tell me about it tonight for my
bedtime story please?"

"Oh, that's not fair, I want to know too," Tim's mum objected.

"Ok, ok!" Pete laughed.

"When Tim's finished eating and I've showered we will all go
upstairs, and you can both lie down on Tim's bed, and I will tell you
both all about it. But now I am taking a shower!" And with that
Pete ran upstairs.

Tim's eyes were gleaming in the kitchen light.
"Mum, do you really think it is an important piece of surfing history,
or is dad joking?"

"Don't look so serious darling!" laughed Tim's mum. "If he is
joking I am going to throw it out and that is that!"

Pete got out of the shower and looked around the house for his wife
Mary. Not finding her he went to Tim's room. They were both
lying on the bed, and when he opened the door they both pretended
to be fast asleep.

"Oh, too tired for a story are you?"

"NO!" shouted Tim as he shook his mum awake. "Tell us about that funny snapped surfboard thing dad!"

"Ok, ok, are you both comfy? Then I'll begin."

"I was surfing in Indonesia, about 25 years ago, I was only young and it was my first trip to Indonesia. I didn't have much money, but I had met another surfer called Waxer, and we were living in a hut on the beach.

We surfed at first light and then later on as the wind changed direction we would paddle back in and get some fishing lines. We would spend the rest of the day fishing, and then later on as the sun set and the winds went back off shore we would surf the evening glass.

Later we would make a fire on the beach and cook the fish we had caught.

Life was easy and slow. Waxer spoke Indonesian well, and once a week we would go and buy water and fruit from the market.

We lived like this for nearly a month, both of us getting more confident and better at surfing. The waves were getting bigger and bigger each day. By the end of that month we both felt like we were capable of surfing any waves that Hui (the god of the sea) could throw at us.

Lots of locals would come and watch us surfing, back then there were probably only ten surfers on the whole island!

The equipment we were using was very different to the things you have today. The boards were over ten feet long, and super thick. When we had finished surfing we would drag the boards up the beach and leave them outside the hut. No-one could steal them; no-one else could even pick them up!!

We didn't have leashes back then, so if you lost your board you had to swim back to the beach and try and get to your board before it got smashed on the rocks!

Waxer and I both had to repair our boards and we got pretty good at it. One day Waxer and I paddled out and the waves were a bit smaller. We were playing on the waves seeing who could hang ten the longest, and Waxer had a killer ride. I tried to beat him, but I fell off, and my board got washed straight on to the rocks. I swam straight to it, but it was too late.

My surfboard had been broken in two!! Waxer paddled back in and we both looked at my poor board.

"What can we do?" asked Waxer.

"Well we can't fibreglass it back together; we don't have enough resin. But I reckon I could seal the end so it is water tight. What do you think buddy?"

"It will be too short to surf on," replied Waxer, "But we don't have much choice!"

Waxer went fishing, and when the board had dried out in the sun I shaped what was left of the front of the board in to a pointy nose and covered it in resin.
My friend came back and surveyed my handiwork.

"Nice job, looks ok, I wonder what she will surf like mate?"

We ate our fish supper and talked about how we thought the surfboard would surf. Waxer said that it would sink when I got on it, but I didn't think so.

We woke early and I checked the board. It was ready for its maiden voyage!

Waxer paddled out next to me but he kept having to wait for me.

"It doesn't paddle as fast as your board," I called out.

When a wave came I soon found that I could sink my board under it and pop up on the other-side much like a cormorant. Finally we were both sitting on our boards and Waxer called me on to the next wave.

WOW!! The board was super-fast and turned really easily, I could do turn after turn, and even Waxer couldn't carve like I could on my new board.

We surfed all day swapping boards and we saw the shorter board as a challenge. Once you were up and riding it was ace, but it was a bit harder to catch the waves.

We shared boards for a week and then it was time for me to fly home. We had some arak which we were given by some friendly locals, and on my last night Waxer and I shared the bottle.

I woke the next morning with a headache, and no surfboard!! Someone had taken my shorter board in the night. Luckily Waxer's board was still there.

I flew home with this little piece of my longboard that I had cut off and some great memories of surfing with a cool Australian.

It took surfers ten more years before surfboard designers realised that you could ride shorter, more manoeuvrable surfboards that were easier to duck under the waves. If I had only realised what I had discovered I would have been the person to start the short board revolution, but an Australian surfer called Bob Mctavish got credited with the discovery of short boards about five years later. That piece of 'junk' as you call it, is all that I have left to prove that I was possibly the first surfer to ride a short board. And that Tim is why I don't want your mother to throw it away."

"Oh it looks like Tim has fallen asleep, but I liked your story, and I will let you keep your invaluable piece of history, but only if you keep it in the garage where it belongs!"

"You drive a hard bargain honey, but ok."

And with that Pete and Mary climbed off Tim's bed and flicked the light switch off.

"Goodnight sweetheart, Goodnight" called Mary and Pete, but Tim couldn't hear. He was far away riding wave after wave on a deserted island.

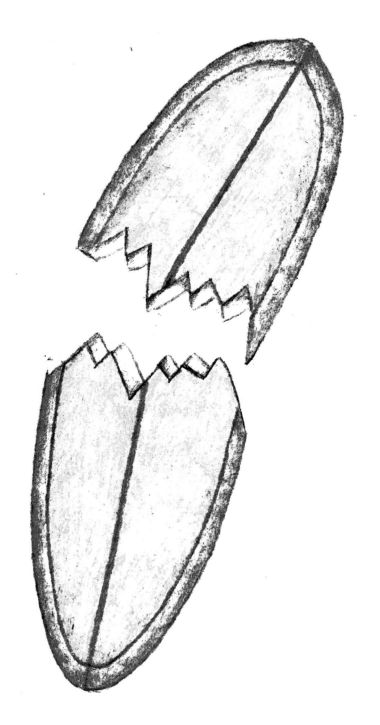

Malibu Madness

Tim walked into the garage to get his pushbike out.

"Hi Dad. Is it ok if I ride round to the beach please?"

"Sure Tim but before you go can you tell your mum that it's going to take me another half hour to glass this fin back in to my Malibu-board.".

Tim looked at the longest board in his dad's board rack. "Ok dad. Are you going to ride your Malibu-board this weekend?"

"I think so if I can finish it in time"

"What fin are you putting in?" Tim asked.

Pete opened a big black metal box, and inside Tim saw ten or more fins.

"No way dad, are they all surfboard fins - even this one?" laughed Tim holding up a fin with a large flat aeroplane wing on the tip of the fin.

"You may laugh young man, but that fin helped me win the first Hotdoggers Malibu Classic competition back in 1975!

"You mean you actually surfed with it? It doesn't even look like a proper fin. How did you win with that thing?" questioned Tim.

"You run along and tell your mother that I'll be half an hour and I'll tell you all about it after we've had supper".

"Ok Dad," and Tim cycled off up the path towards the kitchen.

By the time Tim had got back from the beach Pete had glassed the fin back onto the Malibu-board and was sitting down in the kitchen talking to Mary.

"Was the beach still there Tim?" Pete joked.

"Dad stop being silly! I still don't believe that you surfed with that weird aeroplane fin thing, and I definitely don't think you could have actually won a competition with it".

"If you eat all your supper I'll even show you my trophy, Tim."

"Cool. What's for supper, Mum?"

"Sprouts, peas, carrots and lentils," answered Mary and Mary and her husband laughed at the look of horror on Tim's face!!

After supper while Tim was in the shower, Pete went in to the attic to get the trophy. He even managed to find a couple of newspaper cuttings and photos.

"OK, Dad" shouted Tim, "I'm in bed."

Pete came into Tim's room carrying a big golden trophy and the newspaper cuttings.

"Are you ready then, little man? Then I'll begin. Surfing was a very new sport back in the 70's. In fact it was often difficult to find other people to surf with! At our local beach there were only about 10 surfers, but we had heard of other groups of surfers down in Cornwall and a group up in Wales. If a new surfer came to the beach it would really be something. Everyone would crowd round and ask where they were from and how many people were surfing there.

One day I was driving to the beach with my board on the roof and I saw a hitch-hiker with a surfboard. Of course, I stopped and picked him up and by the time we got to the beach we were the best of friends. He even stayed at my house for 2 nights. He was from France and he told me about their waves and the surf scene and when we went for a surf he had a truly unique style. We stayed together for a few days and then he moved on.

The local paper had heard about this French surfer and sent a reporter down to the beach. He was disappointed that he had missed 'Frenchie' as we called him but said he would still like to run a story about surfing.

All the local guys were arguing about who was the best, when the reporter said, "Why don't you guys organise a competition; the

Journal will put up the prizes. We get a great story, and you guys find out who is the best"

We all jumped at the idea. All we had to do was work out how to judge who was the best.

Someone said how about the longest ride, another person said how about the best move and no-one could agree.

Surfing is a very difficult sport to judge:- no-one crosses the finishing line first; no-one scores more goals; it's a very personal sport.

In the end we all decided to form a surf club called the Hotdoggers and the competition would be who could hang five the longest. Hanging five is when you walk down the board and put five toes over the nose (if you hang ten it's both feet!)

The date for the competition was set, and everyone had three weeks to get ready.

Everyone wanted to win the competition, and the Journal had said they would give five pounds to the winner and a big trophy.

Five pounds was a lot of money back in 1975, and all the guys took it very seriously.

Everyone was busy practising hanging five, and I got pretty good!

Some guys started altering their boards so it was easier to hang five. People stuck bricks on the tail of their board so that when they walked to the nose their weight at the front was balanced by the brick at the back!!

People made really big fins, made the nose of their boards bigger.- anything for a longer nose ride!

A week before the competition the waves got pretty big, and more experienced surfers were getting really long rides, maybe thirty seconds on the nose hanging five! I was up there with the best of them and I thought if I was lucky I might have a chance at the competition.

Six days later disaster struck! My fin somehow snapped, and I didn't have another one. I couldn't surf in the competition.

I drove home from the beach feeling disappointed and hard done by.

As I drove round the corner I noticed smoke coming out of my chimney. Strange I thought, I hadn't lit a fire, maybe one of my friends had called round.

I pulled up outside and walked to the door. Looking through the window I saw Frenchie asleep by the fire!!

I had told him to call round if he was ever passing by, and to let himself in and make himself at home, which he obviously had!!

Frenchie woke up when I came in, and after he had told me about his travels around Cornwall and the waves he had surfed I told him about the competition, and then about my fin snapping.

He looked at my snapped fin, and stood silently for a minute, obviously weighing something up in his head. Then with a shrug he opened his rucksack and pulled out the weirdest looking fin in the whole world!!

It was longer than most fins, but the most unusual feature was that on the very tip of the fin was what looked like an aeroplane wing! The wing had a lip down each of the narrow sides, and the wing was curved not totally flat.

He went on to explain that it was designed for nose-riding, and that the wing shape held the surfboard in the wave so that when you walked to the nose the tail stayed in the wave, and that made it possible to steer the board from the nose.

He gave the fin to me as a gift saying he would have had to sell it to get back to France anyway because his mum had fallen ill.

We glassed the fin on to my board, and when we had finished I offered to drive Frenchie to the ferry port.

I drove through the night and we got there just as the lorries were boarding for the 6am crossing. Frenchie climbed on to a lorry and I waved goodbye and wished him Bon Voyage!!

Looking at my watch I realised the competition was starting at twelve noon:- I had to be at the beach in six hours!!

I raced home, and made it by ten o'clock.

Quickly eating some bread I put my board on the car and drove to the beach.

I had half an hour before the competition started, so I paddled out for a few waves. The fin was awesome!! I could walk to the nose of the board and still steer the board!

All of the Hotdoggers lined up on the beach with their surfboards behind them. The photographer took a picture and then we split in to two groups of five surfers.

I was in the second heat, and while the first heat was paddling out everyone was looking at my fin. Basher had the longest nose ride in the first group, twenty eight seconds, and went through to the final.

I paddled out in the second group, had one nose ride all the way to the beach and walked up to the judges. Thirty two seconds! I knew no-one would beat me, so I sat next to Basher and waited for the whistle.

Eventually it blew and I was in the final against Basher.

We paddled out together, talking about how the paper would represent the sport of surfing. Some of the guys in my heat said it was an unfair advantage to have my fin, and that I had cheated. I pointed out that they had stuck house bricks on their boards, but they didn't see it the same way.

When Basher and I were out the back I told him to catch a wave on my board and try out the fin. We swapped boards and off he went. Thirty four seconds on the nose!!

He paddled back and we swapped back. I caught a wave. Thirty six seconds.

Basher had another go:- thirty five seconds.

I had one more wave and this one I rode all the way to the sand on the nose:- forty one seconds!!

Basher couldn't beat me and I was the winner!!! No-one could say I had had an unfair advantage and everyone congratulated me, especially when I gave the prize money to the surf club treasurer!

The reporter from the Journal wrote a great story about us, and I got my picture in the paper.

The article did a lot to spread the understanding of surfing, and more people got interested in the sport.

Tim looked at the trophy with sleepy eyes.

"I'm going to win a trophy for surfing one day dad."

"Well you better get some sleep then Tim and tomorrow we will go surfing."

"Can I try your Malibu board?"

"Sure you can," answered Pete, and reaching the door stopped to turn off the light,

"Goodnight" whispered Pete, but Tim didn't hear him. He was dreaming of Malibu surfing and hanging five.

Stand On Your Own Two Feet!

Tim came running up the garden path with his best friend Steve. It was a Friday night and Steve was going to stay over.

Steve had stayed over before, but this was the first time that Tim's dad was going to take them both surfing in the morning.

I am sure that you are well aware that Tim is a good young surfer, but Steve had never been surfing before and was a little bit nervous.

After supper (sausage and mash, Tim's favourite), Tim asked his dad how he first learnt to surf.
"I learnt in Devon; I didn't have anyone to teach me." laughed Pete.
"In fact I had to surf otherwise I might have drowned."
"What board were you using?" Steve chipped in.
"I was using a wooden board," Pete answered with a faraway look in his eye.
"You told me you kept all of your surfboards Dad," said Tim in-between gulps of ice-cream.
"I did," replied Pete.
"It's not in your surfboard rack Dad, otherwise I would have asked you a story about it."
"Ah, but it is my surfboard rack, I made it out of my old surfboard!" laughed Pete.
"No way Dad, and you never told me!" exclaimed Tim
"You built a board rack out of your first wooden surfboard, will you tell me and Steve about how you learnt to surf on it tonight before bed please Dad ?"
"OK, OK, give me a call when you are ready for bed and I will tell you all about it," smiled Pete as he started to eat his ice cream.

"OK dad," shouted Tim from the bedroom, "We're ready!"
Pete smiled and walked up the stairs.
"Are you both comfy? Then I'll begin," he said as he sat down.

When I was a teenager my father got me a job working on the boat which sailed to Lundy Island, just off the Devonshire coast. It was the first time I had been on a real boat and I really enjoyed it. Sometimes the crossing would be rough, but it never bothered me, and when everyone else was being sick I would try and stand up without holding on to anything, practising my balance.

The population of Lundy Island is only about 28 now, but back then it was even smaller and the houses they lived in were very basic.

One day a lady got on board to sail back to the mainland. She sat on her own on the boat and after we set sail I stopped to talk to her. She told me all about the massive seal population which lived on the other side of the island and how she enjoyed watching them from her kitchen window.

About a week later she got back on board to return to Lundy. She had a big heavy bag with her and as she was on her own I offered to carry it off the boat for her when we docked.

I noticed no one waiting for her on the island, so I offered to carry it to her house.

This was the start of a great friendship that was to last almost five years. When we arrived at her house I saw that it was in a sorry state. Her husband had died ten years earlier and the house was in serious need of some repair work.

We sat and drank tea and watched the seals play in the waves from the kitchen window. When it was time to go I thanked her for the tea and promised to visit her again.

I went to see her twice a week, always taking a packet of biscuits for us to share with the tea and we would watch the seals.

It was the end of summer now and the weather was starting to get worse. On one visit I noticed that the floor was wet and the lady told me that the roof had a small hole in it. I went to look at the hole and it was about nine feet long and a foot wide! Hardly small!! I said I would try to bring some wood round to fix it the next day before the winter storms came.

When we set sail back to Ilfracombe harbour on the mainland, I told the captain about the hole. He said I could bring some wood to repair the old lady's roof. I told my dad when I got home and he said I would need to be quick, because a storm was due to hit and if I didn't fix it soon, he thought the roof would blow off if the wind got under it.

I found a bit of plywood which looked about the right size, and cleaned it up. The front was bent up a bit and it wasn't quite flat. The edges were rounded off not square, but it was the only wood I had, and that was that.

That night I couldn't sleep, the wind was blowing and I kept thinking of my friend on Lundy Island all on her own.

When the sun came up I ate breakfast and made my way down to the harbour. It was so hard to carry the wood, the wind kept blowing it. Finally I made it to the ship and the captain helped me get the wood on board.

"We have no passengers today," he shouted against the wind.

My face fell.
"Are we going to sail?"
"It's very stormy, and it hasn't hit yet. It's up to you."

"I am worried about the old lady, when the storm hits her roof will blow off unless I repair it first."
"OK Pete, we'll sail, but no complaining when you get scared or feel sick."
"Ha!" I laughed, but I didn't feel so confident.

The captain eased the boat out of Ilfracombe harbour into the Bristol Channel. The waves were crashing in to the bow of the boat, and the wind was blowing the spray straight in to my eyes. It was impossible to see where we were going and we weren't even in the Channel proper yet.

"Pete, tie some rope through the hole in that bit of wood of yours and tie the other end around the mast."

"Aye aye sir!" and I made the wood fast.

"Now get below deck until I call you back up!" ordered the captain.

I ran below deck and was sick as a dog. I lost all track of time; all I wanted was to be back in bed.

I heard someone calling my name and remembering where I was, I ran up the stairs back to the captain.

"It is too rough to go in to the harbour. We'll have to turn around and go back."

"What about the lady?" "What about the roof?"

"Forget the lady, forget ......" But the captain didn't finish his sentence. The engine had died. I watched the captain struggle to start it again. "Untie that rope from your bit of wood and tie yourself on to the mast!" ordered the captain.

For some reason I didn't want the bit of wood to be lost, so I tied it to me instead of the mast. I watched as we drifted around the island. The captain seemed very frightened, saying there were lots of hidden reefs.

I noticed a light on the top of the cliff. It was the old lady's house.

"Try and aim for the light," I shouted. "There's a gap in the reef."

Just as I finished shouting a rogue wave hit the boat, and I was swept off the ship and went under water for what felt like minutes, but was probably only seconds. When I surfaced I pulled the rope I had tied around my waist and felt my plank of wood next to me. I clambered on to the wood and saw a wave about to hit me. I paddled my arms and when the wave hit me I shot forward. I had lost sight of the light, so I stood up on the wood in order to be able to see over the white water.

"There it was!"

I leaned my weight to the right and steered towards the light. The wood stopped suddenly and I fell off. I could stand up on dry land! I waded out of the sea on to the beach, and there was my friend, the old lady with a big lamp.

"And what are you doing surfing on a day like this young man?"

"I have just been washed overboard from that boat. Look, the captain is in trouble."

We stood and watched the captain struggling to keep the boat pointing towards the waves, waiting for the moment when the ship would surely smash in to the reef. Just as we were certain he would run aground the faint sound of an engine kicked in, and slowly, slowly, the captain eased away from the razor sharp reef.

Eventually we lost sight of the boat's running lights and we turned and made our way back to the house.

"I hope the captain's OK," I frowned.

The old lady, Rose, seeing that I was scared and suffering from shock, told me a story of her travels to Hawaii whilst tucking me in to bed.

"When I arrived in Hawaii I was treated to a surfing display," finished Rose.
"What is surfing?" I asked.
"Just what you did when you rode that wood to the beach standing up and I think you are a natural and must certainly carry on the sport!"
"What about your roof?" I asked. Just then there was rapping on the front door and the coastguard came in.

He was glad to see me and listened to our story of me 'surfing'. He told us that the captain had radioed to report a man overboard.

He stayed for a cup of tea and then went back to report that I was safe and well.

My story was in all the national papers and with all the publicity I was getting, a wood company sponsored the mending of Rose's roof, so she was happy. I got to surf on my plank every day, much to people's amazement.

"And that, boys, is how I learnt to stand on my own two feet."
"Boys, Boys," but the boys were asleep dreaming of all the waves they would ride in the morning.

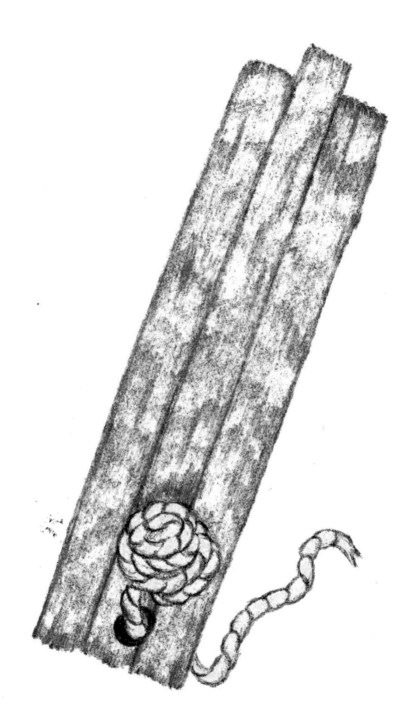

Tim Saves The Day

Tim had been surfing on his dad's Malibu board for most of the day. He found it hard to turn the big board at first, but now, after nearly three hours of solid surfing, he was getting the hang of it.

The surfboard was just over nine feet (three metres) long, more than twice the height of Tim.

His dad had carried the board down to the water's edge at eight thirty and now, at eleven thirty, the tide was nearly all the way in.

Tim paddled for a wave. I say wave, but in truth it was more a ripple. Tim had realised one of the great advantages of long boarding; the bigger the board the easier it is to catch waves.

On his dad's Malibu board two or three strokes and he was flying along; he could catch almost any wave, no matter how small and ride it further, because the wave pushed the board along, even when the wave had broken.

Tim paddled for the wave, popped to his feet and trimmed the board along the wave. He cruised along the wave and, trying to copy his dad's style of surfing, he put one foot in front of the other trying to cross step down the board. Tim promptly fell off the board and popped up next to it, laughing.

When the next wave came, Tim paddled into it and, without standing up, rode the white water to the beach.

He wasn't far from the lifeguard hut now the tide was nearly full. It still took him ages to drag the board up the beach.

Tim put the Malibu board in the shade next to the hut and, turning round, saw his dad.
"I saw you catch more waves today Tim than in a whole week of short boarding!" smiled Pete.
"I really like long boarding dad. You can catch waves that are super small."

"Yes," agreed Pete. "But when the waves get big. I mean really big. (Pete pointed to the roof of the lifeguard hut to show Tim how big he meant) you can catch them on a long board nice and early, so you're up and riding along the wave without having to make a late take-off."
"How do you do that walking down the board thing dad?" asked Tim.
"Cross stepping is what you mean son, and you do it like this."

Pete stood as if he was surfing and then put his back foot in front of his front foot, with the instep facing towards the nose of the board. Then he put his other foot in front and repeated the move again.

Tim watched his dad's feet and had a try himself.
"Watch dad." shouted Tim, and started cross stepping down the beach.
"Good Tim. Try it on the wall by the café now. If you can make if all the way around the café I will buy you an ice-cream."
"We get them free from mum anyway." laughed Tim, but he ran over to the low wall and started practising.
After a few falls, he made it.
"Good son. Now try cross stepping backwards as if you were walking back down the board."
Pete laughed as Tim fell off the wall again and again.
"It's so hard going backwards, I will never be able to do it!" groaned Tim.
"Slowly, slowly my boy. Rome wasn't built in a day. Take a break and try again later!"

Tim went and had some lunch in the café. It took ages to get his lunch from his mum, Mary. There were loads of tourists visiting the beach today and, when she finally got around to Tim, she looked tired.

"Hey mum, guess what? I've learnt to cross step!" said Tim proudly.

"That's great darling. Listen Tim; the girl who helps out on Sundays couldn't come today. Can you help me with the washing up later please?"
Tim looked at his mum.

"I've got someone from the tourist board coming to do a write-up about the beach today and I want the place to be clean and tidy." finished Mary.
Tim frowned. "Can I do the dishes in a couple of hours when the tide's gone out a bit, please mum?"

Mary laughed out loud. "You sound just like your father Tim. Of course you can. It's twelve thirty now, be back by three please. They said that they would be here around four o'clock."
"Cool! Thanks mum. Do you want a hand with the people now?"
"No, you're a good lad. Off you go but don't be late!" waved Mary, as Tim ran back to the Malibu board.

Tim didn't have so far to drag the board now the tide was fully in. It was a spring tide, which meant that the water was as high as it ever got. There was only a thin strip of beach showing. It was difficult to see the sand because there were so many families on the beach!

Tim dodged through the crowds and, reaching the water's edge, stopped and put his leash on.

He paddled out in the rip current so that he didn't have to go through the waves and, looking at the rocks, he marvelled at how fast they were whizzing by.

He paddled across the rip current towards the line-up of other surfers and sat waiting his turn.

Tim had been surfing for what seemed like twenty minutes but it was in fact an hour, when he heard three blasts of a whistle on the beach.

It was a lifeguard signal. One blast was to attract people's attention. Two blasts were to attract other lifeguards' attention and three blasts meant lifeguards taking action.

Tim looked around but couldn't see anyone in trouble. He watched the lifeguard hut and saw the lifeguards running towards the cliff.

Someone had fallen from the top of the cliff and the lifeguards were running to help, going into their E.A.P. – Emergency Action Plan.

Tim knew what to do in the case of a cliff fall. His dad had made him learn First Aid, C.P.R. and rescue techniques before he was allowed to go surfing without his dad.

Tim also knew that it wouldn't help to rush over. A crowd of people had already gathered to look at the injured person.

Most of the other surfers paddled in to go and watch, so Tim took advantage of the empty line-up and started surfing on all the waves he could catch.

Tim glanced down at his watch and saw with horror that it was already two forty-five. He'd better hurry up or he would be late!

Tim turned to look for a wave to catch to the beach, but there was none coming. In the distance, near the edge of the rocks, Tim thought he saw a shape waving. He carried on watching and felt more certain that there was someone in trouble.

Tim looked back towards the beach; everyone was still crowded around the bottom of the cliff. There was an ambulance there now as well.

Looking back to the shape, he decided he would have to paddle over and check it out.

The Malibu board sped through the water as Tim paddled it into the rip current and out towards where he thought he saw the shape.

As he got nearer he could see it was a boy, frantically swimming against the rip current.

Tim had never done a rescue in real life, but his dad had made him rescue him before and the first time he had pulled Tim off his surfboard when he got close enough and dunked him under water.
"Remember son." his dad had said. "Keep your distance unless you want to be a casualty too!"

Tim stopped five metres away from the boy.
"Help! Help!" shouted the boy. "I'm drowning!"
"Are you on your own?" called Tim.
"Help me! Help me please!" shouted the boy, panicking.
"Ok. Ok, but first tell me, are you on your own?"
"Yes, I am on my own. Please help me. I'm so tired I can't swim properly."
"Ok, just climb onto my surfboard and lie face down. Relax, we're going to be fine."
The boy climbed onto the Malibu board whilst Tim held the board steady in the water.
"What's your name?" asked Tim.

"Rupert. What's yours?"

"Tim. Now listen Rupert, open your legs a bit and slide forward. I'm going to climb on and lie behind you and paddle us in."

After a bit of a struggle, Tim was ready to start paddling.

The current had taken them further out than Tim had ever been before and looking towards the beach, Tim felt the first icy fingers of fear creeping down his back.

"Try and paddle in time with me Rupert." called Tim, trying to sound calm.

"But we're going the wrong way." shouted Rupert.

"No, we have to get out of this strong current before we can start going back in. Now paddle with me." ordered Tim, feeling a bit more confident.

Rupert and Tim paddled for ages. They were making slow progress.

"I can't paddle any more," cried Rupert. "We're going to die."

"No, we're not. I always surf around here," said Tim reassuringly. "Just stay calm and keep paddling. Soon we'll be able to catch a wave towards the beach."

Another fifteen minutes passed and Rupert started to cry.

"I don't think we're any nearer to the beach."

"Yes we are," replied Tim. "I've been taking a mark from the cliff and we're miles nearer to the beach."

Eventually they were close enough to catch a wave to the beach.

"Rupert, we've almost made it. Now listen. Hold onto the edge of the surfboard as hard as you can. We're going to surf a wave in. When you feel the wave take the board, lift you head and shoulders up and arch your back. Ok?" asked Tim.

"Ok." replied Rupert.

Tim looked over his shoulder and, seeing a wave, started to paddle hard. The wave caught the board and Rupert and Tim shot towards the beach. The two boys got washed up the beach and the board tipped over. Standing up, Rupert began to cry again.

"It's ok Rupert, we're safe now. Sit down over here. Did you breathe in any water?"

"No." replied Rupert, sitting down.

"Ok, now come with me. Let's go to the lifeguard hut and see my dad."

Tim helped Rupert up the beach and, seeing his dad walk into the café, Tim called out.

Pete came running over. "Hi Tim, who's your friend?"

"Dad, he nearly drowned. I had to rescue him while you were dealing with the cliff rescue. We were all the way out past the cliff."

Pete looked at his son. "Great job Tim, I will talk to you later. Rupert, come with me to the lifeguard hut and we will get your parents and sort you out."

Pete turned to look back at his son. "Tim go and eat a Mars Bar and have a cup of tea, you look fit to drop."

Pete put his arm around Rupert and led him towards the lifeguard hut.

Tim started walking towards the café. Suddenly he felt very tired and hungry.

Tim walked in through the café door and saw his mum busy behind the counter.

"Where have you been, Tim? You are an hour and a half late. Look at the tables piled high with rubbish. What a mess. Thanks Tim. The one thing I ask you to do and you can't even be bothered to do it."

"But mum…"

"No Tim, just start cleaning up this mess."

Tim started to clear the rubbish off the tables and take the dirty plates into the kitchen. He knew it was pointless trying to tell his mum what had happened; she wouldn't listen.

A man and lady entered the café and walked over to the counter.

"Sorry, we are closed," Mary called to them from the kitchen.

"Yes, we thought you were," the man replied. "We're from the tourist board. We just wanted to say that we liked the beach but that the café wasn't quite up to standard."

"Oh!" replied Mary, "I've had a member of staff away today on important business."

"We will be back next year. If things are better we will recommend you for the…" but the man never finished his sentence. Rupert ran over to him and threw his arms around his dad's neck.

"Not now Rupert!" scolded the man, but looking into his son's face he saw something was wrong, "What's happened? Are you ok?"

Rupert told his dad how he had been swept out to sea and how Tim had saved him on his surfboard. As the story was told, Mary came over to Tim and gave him a hug.

"Sorry for shouting at you," she whispered into Tim's ear.

Tim began to cry and gave his mum a hug.

"It's ok dear. It's ok," soothed Mary, "It doesn't matter. You did the right thing. Your father and I are proud of you."

"I'm sorry about the café mum. I'm sorry," sobbed Tim.

"It's ok dear, it doesn't matter," smiled Mary, drying Tim's eyes.

Pete walked into the café and over to Tim.

"You did a very brave thing today Tim. Well done," congratulated Pete as he swung Tim into the air.

Rupert's dad said: "Look, I'm very grateful for what you have done young man and as far as the café goes, I am glad you were rescuing my son and not helping out in here. I will definitely be recommending that the café and beach go into the tourist guide."

Tim looked at his mum, who was smiling down at him and smiled back.

"Also Tim, I would like to give you a small token of appreciation." and with that, Rupert's dad reached into his pocket, pulled out a ten pound note and offered it to Tim. Tim looked at Pete, who smiling nodded back to him.

"Go ahead Tim, take it. After all, you did save the day."

Tim's New Board

Tim was woken by the gentle shaking of his father.

"Morning son, surf's up!"

Pete never ever came and woke Tim up, especially at 6.30 in the morning!

After a quick cup of tea Pete told Tim to follow him in to the garage. Pete unlocked the door and they both stepped in to the gloomy light. As Tim's eyes adjusted to the dark he saw a bright yellow surfboard next to his wetsuit. It was bigger than his other board, but smaller than his dad's Malibu board.

"Here you go son, a new board built just for you by Little Al. It's a mini Malibu board, built to help you catch as many waves as possible. You'll learn to surf really quickly on this board because you will be able to catch more waves."

"Cool, thanks dad," grinned Tim.

"Let's go then boy!" Pete smiled as he tousled Tim's hair.

As they left the house Tim could hear the waves crashing on the beach.

"How big are the waves, dad?" Tim asked.

"Size doesn't matter Tim, it's all in your head." answered Pete.

They rounded the corner and got their first view of the beach. Solid six foot sets peeled across the bay.

"Dad I can't go surfing in those waves, they're massive!" Tim blurted out.

"Listen Tim, you are the only son I have got, and I promise you I won't let you come to any harm. You have got the skill to surf those waves. You know how the waves work here, you are a fine swimmer, you are only lacking in confidence, and after you have surfed today you will feel more confident, and don't forget I **am** head lifeguard here, and I will be watching you all the way. What do you reckon?"

Tim looked out to the other guys who were sitting on their boards waiting for a set to come. Then he looked along the empty beach, and finally back to his dad.

"If you think that I'll be safe dad, I'll come with you."

"Good lad, let's warm up then son." And with that they started the lifeguards' warm up exercises.

As they got to the edge of the water Tim and Pete put their leashes on.

"Paddle next to me," ordered Pete as he started paddling in an easy rhythm.

Tim was paddling between the rocks and his dad, trying not to worry as they went over bigger and bigger waves. The line up got nearer and Tim started to recognise the faces of his dad's friends.

"Hi Tim, nice to see you," winked Greg as he took off on a beauty.

"Just sit to the outside for a while and tune in to things," said Pete as he swung his long board round and paddled hard for a wave.

Tim watched as his dad took off on what seemed a huge wave. He watched his arms fly above his head as his dad Hung Five! and then saw him do a 'cutback' marvelling at the amount of water his dad sent spraying over the back of the wave on to Greg who was paddling back out for another ride. Pete pulled over the back of the wave next to Greg, and they both fell in to an easy rhythm of paddling with both surfers laughing as they drifted back to the line up.

"Whenever you're ready Tim," called Pete, "GO FOR IT!"

Tim paddled in to the takeoff area."Just relax, don't think too much... enjoy it," encouraged Pete.

"OK, PADDLE SON. HERE YOU GO!"

Tim didn't even look over his shoulder as he normally would. He was afraid that if he saw the size of the wave he would chicken out. He put his head down and paddled as hard as he could.

He felt the wave pick him up, and he popped instinctively to his feet. There was no turning back now, this was it!

He moved forward on the board to gain speed and shot along the wave. He dared not turn, he was going too fast!

Tim crouched low so that he didn't bounce off the board, and turned towards the beach. The wave broke behind him, and the white water (which was twice as high as Tim) spat him out on to the beach.

He undid his leash and walked on to dry sand. He had made it! He noticed that his hands were shaking and that his heart was pounding in his chest, but he loved it! He felt alive and it was great!

He watched his dad catch ten or more big waves and then he came in on the white water.

"You did great out there son, why didn't you come back out? Didn't you like it?"

"Dad I loved it! When I came out my heart was pumping, my hands were shaking. It was the best feeling ever!"

"Son, you can't buy that feeling no matter how much money you have. Some people live for that feeling and nothing else. Most people never experience that feeling in their whole lives. Do you want to hear a story?"
"Sure dad you bet!"

'Well boy, you'll have to wait until bedtime.'

'Oh Dad, that's not fair!'

But Pete wouldn't budge and Tim had to wait until bedtime to hear his dad's story.

Finally it was bedtime; Tim jumped into bed; Pete tucked him in and began to tell his story.

"One day there was a surfer, and he grew bored surfing and looking around the beach he saw a powerful business man taking a walk.

"I wish I could be that important and powerful," he thought, and before he knew what was happening, POW! He became the business man!

He soon got bored being the business man, and when he saw the king being carried along the beach in a big golden chair he thought to himself, "I wish I could be the king."

And before he knew what was happening, POW! He became the king!

He soon grew bored of people bowing in front of him, and being carried around everywhere was a bit boring too. He looked around from his golden chair and saw the sun.
"Ha!" he thought, "What could be more powerful than the sun? I wish I could be the sun."

And before he knew what was happening, POW! He became the sun!

He shone down on all the people, feeling pretty awesome, when all of a sudden a big black cloud blew in front of him blocking out his view of the people.

"That cloud is more powerful than me" he thought. "I wish I could be that cloud."

And before he knew what was happening, POW! He became the cloud!

He enjoyed being the cloud raining down on people, but after a while the wind blew him out to sea.
"AH!" he thought "The wind is the most powerful thing! I wish I could be the wind."

And before he knew what was happening, POW! He became the wind!

He enjoyed being the wind, blowing clouds all over the sky, and then he noticed he was whipping up waves below on the sea.

"AH!" he thought "What could be more powerful than those massive ocean waves? I wish I could be a wave."

And before he knew what was happening, POW! He became a wave.

He travelled across the ocean, feeling all powerful, and wondered what could possibly be more powerful than he was now. As he got closer to the land he noticed people riding waves, harnessing the ocean's mighty power.

"YES!" he thought "They must be the most powerful things, I wish I was a surfer."

And before he knew what was happening, POW! He became a surfer again.

Tim rubbed his sleepy eyes.

"That was cool dad! I am always going to be a surfer. I am never going to stop. What's the point in doing anything else?"

Pete smiled at his son,

'I know what you mean, Tim. I have felt the same way my whole life. Surfing is a lot more than just riding waves'.

Pete flicked the light off. 'Sleep well, Tim. Tim? Tim?'

But Tim didn't answer. He was asleep dreaming of surfing.

Tim's First Ding

It was the second week of Tim's summer holiday. He had spent the first twelve days surfing on the beach where his dad was head lifeguard.

Each day he would go to work with Pete and surf all day, only stopping for lunch and the occasional ice-cream which his mum Mary gave him from the cafe she owned.

Life was looking pretty good, especially as he had another six weeks of school holidays to go, and a new boy whom he had met was going to come to the beach today with his surfboard.

Tim had been surfing for about half an hour when he saw Rob paddling out.

"Hi Rob!" called Tim as Rob paddled towards him.

Tim watched as Rob, (who didn't even glance at Tim) paddled straight past him. He turned and caught the wave Tim had been paddling into position for.

Tim waited for Rob to paddle back out and tried again:
"Nice wave Rob," nodded Tim.

"Yeah I suppose it was, maybe I'll let you get some waves later when I'm tired- watch out!" added Rob as he paddled past Tim, turned and rode off on Tim's wave.

Rob carried on taking nearly all the waves for the rest of the morning.

When Tim had had enough he turned to Rob and said "I'm going for lunch, see you later," and paddled in.

Tim was talking to his dad by the cafe about how Rob had taken all the waves, when Rob walked up to him. When he found out that Pete was the head lifeguard and Tim's dad he totally changed.

"Yeah if you could watch me surf later after lunch you might be able to recommend me to a company for sponsorship," shouted Rob.

"Yes ok Rob. Nice to meet you, I will watch you surfing and see if there is anyone I can think of who might like to sponsor you." And with that Pete winked at Tim and walked towards an old lady who was looking lost.

Tim and Rob had lunch in the cafe, and Rob spent the whole time telling Tim how he was sure he was good enough for a company to sponsor him, and about his latest moves.
"Don't worry Tim, I can remember when I was just a beginner; in a few years you will be able to catch waves too!"

Tim was lost for words. How dare Rob say that! He turned and walked to his board outside the door and started back down the beach towards the sea.

As Tim paddled out through the surf Rob paddled over and started taking all the waves again.

Tim could see his dad watching them through the binoculars, but he couldn't manage to catch a single wave before Rob paddled round him and "stole" the wave.

Eventually a perfect wave wrapped towards Tim. He could see the glassy wall curving over the sandbank, and he knew he was going to catch the biggest and best wave of the day. He paddled three or four times and felt his mini Malibu board speed in to the wave. He popped to his feet and dropped down the wave face. He bent his knees and crouched as he carved a sharp bottom turn and angled the board back towards the top of the wave. Looking up towards the top of the wave he saw the head of Rob and the nose of his board.

Rob was paddling as hard as he could to get into the wave. Tim watched helplessly as Rob's board smashed in to his new board.

"You idiot, look where you are going, I was going to catch that wave then!" shouted Rob.

Tim paddled back to the beach and looked at his board.

There was a long gash all the way across the nose of the board on the bottom, and worse, the rail had a big cut all the way through it.

Tim thought his dad would be upset because the board was only a couple of week old, and had cost nearly two hundred pounds. Pete came walking over.

"Are you alright son?"

"I am dad, but look what's happened to my new board- it's ruined!"

Pete looked at the damage and seeing that Tim was about to cry pulled a silly face.

"Dad stop it! It's not funny, my board's ruined!"

"No it's not. We'll dry it out now and after work we can fix it in the garage, and you can surf on it tomorrow".

"I won't get any waves if Rob comes down anyway. HE takes all the waves!"

"Ah yes, we'll have to see about that," reflected Pete.

"Now Tim, go and put the board on the grass next to the lifeguard hut and I'll see you up there. Put the kettle on."

Pete turned and began to patrol the beach, and Tim picked the board up and carried it towards the lifeguard hut. As Pete patrolled the beach Rob came running over.

"Did you see me surfing? Was I good? I'm better than Tim. Did you see how many waves I caught?"

"Yes Rob I did. I think I might know someone who would like to see you surf, can you come down here tomorrow morning, say seven thirty?"

"Thanks Paul, I knew I was good enough," nodded Rob.

"My name's Pete, and we will see about that tomorrow," said Pete as he turned and carried on his beach patrol.

After Pete finished work he took Tim straight to his garage. Pete showed Tim how to cut off the damaged part of the rail put new foam inside and then how to shape it and fibreglass it in to place.

When they had finished mending the rail and nose of Tim's new board they had supper and then Pete told Tim what his plan was to stop Rob being such a greedy surfer.

Pete said that after they had checked on the board and Tim was in bed he was going to call his friend Ashley, and get him to go to the beach to meet Rob in the morning. Ashley was going to tell Rob that he was a scout from Tiki,(the surfboard and wetsuit company) and then they would go for a surf together.

Ashley was the under eighteen's British long board champion, and was a top surfer.

"Ashley won't let Rob get a single wave and then," finished Pete. "I shall have a little chat with Rob!"

Tim had experienced his father's little chats before, and smiled at the thought of Rob being on the receiving end of one.

They checked the board, and Tim said goodnight to his parents.

"No bedtime story tonight dear?" questioned Mary.

Pete explained all about Rob and how Tim's new board was damaged. Then he went on to explain about his plan for the morning.

"Oh dear!" frowned Mary," I don't like the sound of Rob much."

"Don't worry honey, I will phone Ashley in a minute, and after tomorrow everything will be fine. Just you wait and see!"

Rob woke up early; six o'clock. He got dressed and made his board and wetsuit ready. Today was his big day and he wanted everything to go well. After he had eaten his breakfast he woke his mum. She got dressed and after a cup of tea, drove an eager Rob down to the beach.

Rob said good-bye to his mum and gave her a kiss.

"Good luck, darling" waved his mum as Rob walked across the car park looking for the person Pete had told him to meet.

Rob saw the only person on the beach with a surfboard and walked over to him.

Pete and Tim could see Rob walking over to Ashley from their vantage point on the cliff, but they couldn't hear what they were saying.

They watched as the two paddled out in the surf together. Rob turned and lined up a wave. Just as he was going to start paddling Ashley snaked around Rob and caught the wave. Tim laughed out loud.

"Now he will get a taste of his own medicine," smiled Tim to his dad.

For the next half hour poor Rob never even caught a single wave, even though he paddled for most of them!

"Look they're paddling in," pointed Pete. "Tim you go and finish off the sanding on your board like I showed you, and I will go and have a chat with Ashley and Rob."

Tim turned and started to jog back to the garage. I wouldn't like to be in Rob's shoes now he thought.

"You never missed a single wave," sighed Rob. "I never even got one!"

"Not to worry," smiled Ashley "I can remember when I was a beginner too." The words stung Rob, but there was nothing he could say in his defence. Now he knew how Tim had felt yesterday.

Pete jogged over to the two surfers just as Ashley walked away.

"How did it go Rob? What did Ashley say?" asked Pete.

"I don't know," said Rob. "I just don't know."

"Listen Rob, you know you asked me to watch you surf yesterday.

Well I watched you in the morning and the afternoon. You are good at surfing, but you knew that didn't you?"

"I thought so," replied Rob.

"Good at surfing," continued Pete, "but you are not a good surfer."

"But I thought you just said...." interrupted Rob.

"I said you are good at surfing, and you are, but Rob you are a bad waterman. You show no respect for others, you are a danger in the water as you proved by dropping in on Tim yesterday, and I am not surprised that Ashley didn't give you the deal. There will always be someone better than you. If you treat others badly then don't be surprised if others treat you the same way. I think you have the potential to be a really good surfer, but it's not about catching as many waves as you can. Try and remember that and I am sure that you will go a long way."

"Ok I will try and remember what you have told me. Thanks for bothering to arrange the meeting with Ashley. I am sorry if I have been behaving like an idiot. Look, can I pay for the damage to Tim's board or something?"

"Just remember what I have said and try to act on it. If you do, that will be payment enough."

"Ok I will, thanks," said Rob as he walked off slowly towards his mum's car.

After a little chat Rob's mum drove off and Rob walked back down the beach, and paddled out next to Tim.

Tim saw Rob coming and thought oh no! But when Rob paddled out he appeared quite different.

"Morning Tim, how's it going?"

"Uh, good I think, thanks" replied Tim cautiously.

"Look, your wave!" called Rob.

Rob watched as Tim took off. When Tim paddled out he watched Rob catch a wave. Pretty soon the two boys were cheering each other in to the waves, and laughing when one of them fell off!

Tim looked at his watch. "Blimey Rob it's lunchtime already!"

"Oh no!" exclaimed Rob, "My mum forgot to give me any lunch money!"

"No worries mate!" grinned Tim "My mum will sort us out. Come on!"

After lunch had gone down Tim and Rob headed out for one last surf before Rob's mum came to pick him up.

On the last wave Tim dropped in on Rob and they rode the wave side by side all the way to the beach.

"That was the best surf ever!" laughed Rob.

"Yeah for sure," agreed Tim.

Pete walked towards the two friends.

"Nice surfing boys! Great stuff!!" he smiled.

"Hey Tim, I will try and get my mum to bring me down tomorrow, do you fancy another surf together?"

"Yeah for sure! I will be here from eight. See you tomorrow morning!"

"Cool. See you tomorrow Tim," called Rob as he picked his board up and started to walk towards the car park.

"BYE ROB!" shouted Tim.

Pete and Tim picked up his repaired surfboard and started to walk back towards their house.

"How was the board? Were the repairs ok?" asked Pete.

"Yes dad the repairs were fine. Listen, I caught loads of good waves and so did Rob...." Tim started to tell Pete all about the waves that he and Rob had caught, and before he knew it they were back in their garden.

Mary looked up from the flowerbed that she was weeding and listened to Tim's excited chatter.

"So the day went well did it?" she asked Pete with a smile on her face. Pete nodded in reply and Tim turned to look at his mum;

"Mum, can my friend Rob stay for tea tomorrow please?"

"Well dear we'll have to see, we'll have to see" and with that Mary smiled. She was glad that Tim had found a new friend to surf with.

Barrel Boy

'Heavy' was the word he would use to describe it. The waves were falling in one go from top to bottom, crashing down, peeling from left to right. He could hear the air 'crack' as it was forced out of the hollow waves. No one was on the beach; no one was in the water.
Tim had been training for a day like this all of his short surfing life. For two years now he had gone out most days, rain or shine, messy or clean. Some of his friends talked a good wave, wore all the latest threads, hell most of them had three or more boards.

Where were they all? he wondered. Should he go out on his own? He had told his dad he wouldn't, but hey, what the old fella didn't know wouldn't hurt him. All or nothing. He knew that was the only way to travel. If he got in he had to be committed. No messing about. 100%. Straight out the back. If he hesitated it could be a world of pain. He shivered at the thought of it. Was he ready?

He was the smallest in his year at school, and as he pulled on his damp wetsuit he felt very small indeed. The tide was nearly all the way in now, and with a short jog Tim was at the water's edge. He stood waving his arms around trying to relax and warm up his shoulders. He bent down and pulled his wetsuit up on his right leg, secured his leash and gave it a good tug.

"OK" he said to himself, and started wading in to the cold water. He shuffled in to the rip by the rocks, and waited in ankle depth for the water to push in before he jumped on the board to paddle out.

Wow. It pushed in all the way up to his waist. Have I bitten off more than I can chew Tim wondered? There was a lot of water moving, it was a spring tide. He waited again, struggling to stand up as the water sucked out back down to ankle level.
"Next time, and I'll go" Tim said to himself.

The water surged in and Tim held his ground. As the level started to drop he jumped on his board and was sucked past the rocks at an alarming rate. No waves were walling up in the rip, because the water current was pulling against the waves, going straight out to sea.

Tim was paddling for all his worth trying to get out the back without getting caught inside. He tried not to look at the waves breaking on his left as he paddled out next to the rocks. He was nearly out now, just starting to feel short of breath. Over the top of the biggest wave he had ever seen in his whole life, and Bingo!! he had made it!

Tim paddled away from the rip current now not wanting to go any further out to sea, being careful to take a mark from the rocks on his left and the car park on the beach so he could tell if he was still drifting.

He could see someone on the beach now. It was difficult to make them out, but they were sitting by the surf life-saving club, where he had been practising his swimming and rescue techniques last summer.

"Good" he said to himself. "If I get in trouble at least someone will know that I am out here."
For the next twenty minutes Tim paddled over the top of waves he wished he had never seen. Ten feet of water sucking up and pitching down is enough to frighten any surfer, let alone a fourteen year old school boy in the water on his own.

I am sure that you have been out in the sea in waves that have made you wish you were back on the beach watching. And when you are out past all the waves, dodging the big ones the last thing you feel like doing is catching one, but as we all know, that is the only way back in!!

Tim was running out of energy. He knew that he couldn't dodge waves like this forever, and that the only way back to the beach was on one of the white capped monsters he had spent the last half hour going over the top of.

He decided to catch one. He scrapped over the top of the last wave in the set, and got in to position. He could feel his heart beating in his chest. He looked towards the beach, and was in place for the last of the three waves.

The wind was strong and offshore, and as he jumped to his feet it tried to hold his board out of the wave. After what seemed like ages he started to drop down the wave, and looking to his left he could see the wave crashing down. Go right he thought. Go right. He started to turn, and looked down the wall of the wave in front of him. It was easily the biggest wave he had ever ridden, over twice his own height. As he flew along the bottom of the wall he could hear the wave catching him up from behind. He cut on to the wall of the wave now, marvelling at the speed water was sucked up and in to the wave. Up and down he carved, desperate to stay ahead of the white water. Time seemed to slow down. Tim could make out patches of foam on top of the water, all the different colours of the sea from grey, green to blue and white. And then it was gone. No more wave. He had outrun the wall. He looked behind him, and saw a small wave of white water coming towards him. He paddled to the beach buzzing.

He undid his leash and walked towards the surf life-saving club and his school stuff. He had never felt like this before. He felt weak in the knees, yet strong. He felt on top of the world. The perfect start to any day he laughed to himself. And what a big wave!! If only someone was there to share it with him. Then he remembered the person he had seen on the beach.

He flicked the hair out of his eyes and looked towards the surf club, and his perfect day was over. The person he had seen was PJ. PJ was the loudest, biggest bully in Tim's year at school.

"Hey maggot!" shouted PJ. "You were lucky out there, thought you might drown!"

"Leave me alone and get away from my stuff!" shouted Tim.

"Oh yeah! And what are you going to do shrimp?!" PJ taunted as he kicked sand on Tim's school shirt and trousers. When Tim got nearer he ran off.

Tim put his clothes on and put his board and wetsuit in the club and grabbed his bag. If he ran he might just be in time for school.

As Tim hurried through the school gates his best friend Rob came over.

"Are you OK Tim?" he asked.
"Yeah, why?" Tim replied.

"PJ said you took a battering at the beach and that you nearly drowned. He said you got caught inside for ages!"
"WHAT! I caught a solid six footer easily. I rode it to the beach. It was awesome, you gotta believe me!"
"Of course I believe you. PJ is an idiot isn't he?!"
"Yeah, what a dork, I can't stand that bully," fumed Tim.

All day long people were coming over to Tim and asking if he was all right. Even worse were the ones who just looked at him and laughed to themselves.

After a brilliant start Tim's day was taking a real turn for the worse.

In the afternoon break Tim and Rob heard PJ talking to his group of friends.

"Have you seen the waves today? Tomorrow will be the same, and I am going to catch me some of that action. Only problem is which board should I ride, my seven five gun, or my eight foot gun. I don't know if I want hard or soft rails, a square or pin tail"

"What a loser!" Tim said to Rob.
Rob nodded his agreement.

"Watch this!" Tim said, and walked over to PJ.
"Hey PJ, going surfing tomorrow are you?"
"Look it's maggot boy!" said PJ. Everyone laughed at Tim.
"Are you coming down to see how it should be done?" laughed PJ.
"No, but I will see you in the water though, bring your friends down PJ and we will see who can really surf," said Tim trying to stop his voice from shaking.

PJ's friends looked at PJ.
"Seven o'clock" PJ said with a slight quiver in his voice. Then the bell went for the last lesson.

On the way home Tim and Rob talked about the morning. As they got nearer the beach they could hear the surf pounding.

"Blimey! That sounds huge, you went out in that?" said Rob.
"Yes, and I got out the back and rode a wave all the way in!" Tim replied with a grin.

"Aren't you scared about tomorrow?" Rob asked his best friend. "Yes, but I know that I am a better surfer than PJ, and hopefully he will stop picking on me if I show him up in front of his friends," replied Tim thoughtfully.

Seven O'clock, and the friends arrived at the beach. PJ was already in his wetsuit with a couple of his gang carrying his board for him.

The two boys checked the surf. The tide was further in than yesterday, the wind was the same as yesterday, and the waves were, if anything, a bit bigger.

PJ was trying to be cool in front of his gang, but Tim could tell he was nervous.

"Want to call it off do you?" jeered PJ.
"Not unless you're scared," replied Tim trying to sound cool.
"No way! Get suited and booted and then we'll see who really is a surfer, Maggot Boy," PJ blustered.

"Look Tim, you know you don't have to do this, you don't have to prove to me that you are a better surfer than stupid PJ, you're miles better!" added Rob.

"Thanks Rob, you're my best mate and I really appreciate you saying that, but I have to put a stop to PJ's bullying, and I think this is my best chance."

"Come on Maggot Boy!" shouted PJ who was now surrounded by an ever increasing number of his friends.

"Gotta go bro," said Tim shaking hands with Rob in the surfers handshake. "Good luck!" was all Rob could say as he watched his best friend walk towards the sea.

Tim and PJ waded up to waist depth and waited. Tim went first despite the size difference between the two boys. As the water sucked back out to sea he jumped on his board and started to paddle, PJ following close behind.
"Hey Maggot, have you checked your leash, it looked like someone had cut it with a knife earlier!"

Tim couldn't turn around now to look at PJ, it was all or nothing. If he turned back now he would get a pounding in the shore break, and besides, everyone on the beach would think he had chickened out.

"You're scum PJ!" was all he could say as he was sucked out to sea in the rip, paddling as fast as he could.

After what seemed like ages Tim felt like he was out past the waves. He turned to look for PJ, but he was no-where to be seen. As he turned back to look out to sea he had the fright of his life.

A wave was in front of him just starting to feather at the top. Seven feet of cold Atlantic juice was just about to crash down on top of Tim! In a flash he was paddling towards the wave. It looked like he might just make it over the wave, but then the top began to fall. Tim kept paddling towards the wave, and the lip of the wave pitched over leaving him inside a little green room of water. He felt the explosion behind him as the wave broke. He held on to his board for all he was worth spinning around and around. His lungs were on fire, he was lost, he didn't know which way was up. He clung to his board knowing it would float. Finally he felt the wave let go of him, and his board shot up and out in to the sweet air. He filled his lungs thankfully, and looked around for the next wave. Luckily for Tim there was a lull between sets, and he paddled out to sea as fast as he could.

Tim sat on his board to regain his breath. He pulled the leash by his ankle, feeding it up through his hands. It was no longer attached to the board!! It had snapped!! Big waves and no leash. No way back to the beach except on a massive wave, and if he fell off he would lose his board and have to swim in. PJ must have cut it nearly all the way through Tim thought. What an idiot. If I had lost my board on that wipe out I could have drowned. Tim fumed inside, how could PJ do such a stupid selfish thing? Where was PJ anyway?

Tim looked around but couldn't see PJ anywhere.
"Time to go in," Tim said to himself.

One chance. No mistakes allowed. If I fall off I am in trouble, but I did it yesterday, and I can do it today.

He paddled for the last wave of a set, but didn't quite catch it. He tried again, and missed the next set wave as well. He was getting closer to the breaking point now. If he went any further it would be impossible to avoid the waves as they formed and threw over.

"Here goes!" Tim shouted as he paddled for another wave.

This time it took him and he felt the massive power in the wave as he flew down the face of it. He was flying along the wave, not able to control the board properly, just crouching down going in a straight line along the wave. He looked over his shoulder and saw that the white water was nearly breaking on top of him. When he turned back to look towards the beach Tim couldn't believe his eyes. He couldn't see the beach, all he could see was the inside of the wave he was riding!!

Wow! I'm inside the wave. The first time I've ever been barrelled, and Rob and PJ will be watching! Just then Tim's world changed. From being on top of the world to being under the sea. The wave overtook Tim and he was swallowed up inside. He lost his board.

He held his breath, and when the pressure eased he swam for the top following the bubbles of air up to the surface. His head came out of the water and he took a quick breath. Then he realised he could stand up. He stood up and waded out of the sea.

Rob had a hold of his board and was looking at Tim's broken leash.

"No way! You snapped your leash in that barrel," Rob shouted over.

"No," said Tim shaking his head "PJ cut it, look it's a clean break. Where is PJ?"

"Over there with his gang." Rob answered.

"What was his wave like, was it better than mine?" Tim asked.

"Mate, he never even caught a wave. You whooped him!"

"Not quite." said Tim as he walked over towards PJ. "I haven't finished yet".

"PJ, I can't believe you cut my leash! I could have drowned out there. I want a word with you!"

"Hey Mag..." But PJ never finished his sentence because Tim had tripped him over on to the sand with a Judo throw.

Tim turned to look at PJ's gang, expecting to be set upon, but instead, they shook their heads looking at PJ on the floor.

"We're sorry for picking on you Tim. PJ is a bully and a liar, are you OK?"

"Yes I'm fine now, thanks," said Tim.

We'll never pick on you or call you names again Tim. Instead we will call you Barrel Boy, after all that was the most amazing barrel ever! See you at break time dude! And with that PJ's gang turned and walked back towards school.

Rob came over to Tim.
"No way!! You got barrelled and made friends with PJ's gang. It's amazing!!"
"I don't care about them," Tim said. "You're my real friend. Come on, let's have a cup of tea in the surf life saving club before school."
"Yeah sure bro," said Rob as they turned towards the club house.
"I'll make it Barrel Boy!" and they both laughed.

About The Author

Merlin Cadogan was a qualified beach lifeguard and surfing instructor for the Tiki surf school in Devon, England.

He has surfed all over the world and has taught hundreds of people to surf.

He wrote most of these stories on surf trips to Indonesia.

Merlin is a professional escapologist and juggler who reached the semi-finals on Britain's Got Talent in 2009, juggling fire underwater and escaping from 10 metres of chain. Merlin is also a keen treasure hunter combining his love of diving with underwater metal detecting and is sponsored by Minelab Metal Detectors.

He has free dived to 30 metres with Sara Campbell and held 2 Guinness World Records for picking the most police handcuffs in one minute and juggling 3 balls underwater the longest.

Connect with Merlin Cadogan

I really appreciate you reading my book! Here are my social media contact details, get in touch!

Find me on Facebook :
https://www.facebook.com/surfstoriesfromtheboardrack

Favourite my Smashwords author page :
https://www.smashwords.com/profile/view/merlin0001

Visit my Website : http://www.merlincadogan.com

Email me : merlincadogan@hotmail.com

Instagram : @merlin_cadogan

Surfing in Westward Ho!

If you are a thinking of trying surfing or are a surfer looking for a new place to enjoy then why not come and check out Westward Ho! in sunny North Devon.

The beach is huge with peaks for miles so it's never crowded. It's a very safe beach with fun waves and a great surfing community that offers encouragement and a warm welcome. Parking is right next to the beach on the beautiful Northam burrows. There are some surf schools offering lessons and all the equipment you need to give surfing a try.

There are lots of quality pubs and restaurants in the village. Pop into Kitemare Surf & Kite shop and say hi to Pete, he will let you know what's going on, where the surf is pumping and where to party!

Unit 3, Latitude 51, Westward Ho!, EX39 1GW

01237 238350

kitemarecompany@gmail.com

www.surfandkiteshop.co.uk